THIS WHERE'S WALLY? BOOK BELONGS TO:

Sarah

HEY, WALLY FANS! FIVE INTREPID TRAVELLERS
ARE LOST IN EVERY SCENE! CAN YOU FIND THEM?

ODLAW   WIZARD   WENDA   WOOF   WALLY
         WHITEBEARD

AND IN EVERY SCENE, THE TRAVELLERS
HAVE EACH LOST SOMETHING PRECIOUS!
CAN YOU FIND THEM TOO?

WALLY'S KEY   WOOF'S BONE   WENDA'S CAMERA

WIZARD WHITEBEARD'S SCROLL   ODLAW'S BINOCULARS

For Wally

First published 1987 by Walker Books Ltd
87 Vauxhall Walk, London SE11 5HJ

This World Book Day collectors edition published 2008

2 4 6 8 10 9 7 5 3 1

© 1987, 1997, 2007 Martin Handford

The right of Martin Handford to be identified as author/illustrator
of this work has been asserted by him in accordance with the
Copyright, Designs and Patents Act 1988.

This book has been typeset in Wallyfont

Printed in China

All rights reserved.

British Library Cataloguing in Publication Data:
a catalogue record for this book
is available from the British Library.

ISBN 978-1-4063-1317-8

www.walkerbooks.co.uk

MARTIN HANDFORD

WALKER BOOKS
AND SUBSIDIARIES
LONDON · BOSTON · SYDNEY · AUCKLAND

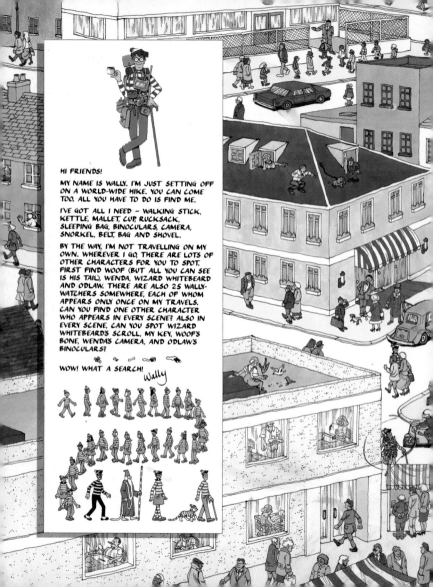

HI FRIENDS!

MY NAME IS WALLY. I'M JUST SETTING OFF
ON A WORLD-WIDE HIKE. YOU CAN COME
TOO. ALL YOU HAVE TO DO IS FIND ME.

I'VE GOT ALL I NEED – WALKING STICK,
KETTLE, MALLET, CUP, RUCKSACK,
SLEEPING BAG, BINOCULARS, CAMERA,
SNORKEL, BELT, BAG AND SHOVEL.

BY THE WAY, I'M NOT TRAVELLING ON MY
OWN. WHEREVER I GO, THERE ARE LOTS OF
OTHER CHARACTERS FOR YOU TO SPOT.
FIRST FIND WOOF (BUT ALL YOU CAN SEE
IS HIS TAIL), WENDA, WIZARD WHITEBEARD
AND ODLAW. THERE ARE ALSO 25 WALLY-
WATCHERS SOMEWHERE, EACH OF WHOM
APPEARS ONLY ONCE ON MY TRAVELS.
CAN YOU FIND ONE OTHER CHARACTER
WHO APPEARS IN EVERY SCENE? ALSO IN
EVERY SCENE, CAN YOU SPOT WIZARD
WHITEBEARD'S SCROLL, MY KEY, WOOF'S
BONE, WENDA'S CAMERA, AND ODLAW'S
BINOCULARS?

WOW! WHAT A SEARCH! *Wally*

GREETINGS,
WALLY FOLLOWERS!
WOW, THE BEACH WAS
GREAT TODAY! I SAW
THIS GIRL STICK AN
ICE-CREAM IN HER
BROTHER'S FACE, AND
THERE WAS A SAND-
CASTLE WITH A REAL
KNIGHT IN ARMOUR
INSIDE! FANTASTIC!

Wally

TO:
WALLY FOLLOWERS,
HERE, THERE,
EVERYWHERE.

WHERE'S ON THE BEACH WALLY

IT'S ME AGAIN, WALLY FOLKS!
SOME VERY STRANGE THINGS
WERE HAPPENING AT THE
AIRPORT THIS MORNING.
A HELICOPTER CHOPPED ALL
THE FLAGPOLES DOWN;
A SMUGGLER WAS CAUGHT
HIDING WATCHES IN HIS
BEARD; A HERD OF ELEPHANTS
WAS GETTING ONTO A JUMBO.
WEIRD!

Wally

TO:
WALLY FOLKS,
UNDER THE CARPET,
UNDER THE BED,
DOWN UNDER.

WHEN
=AIRPORT
WALLY?=

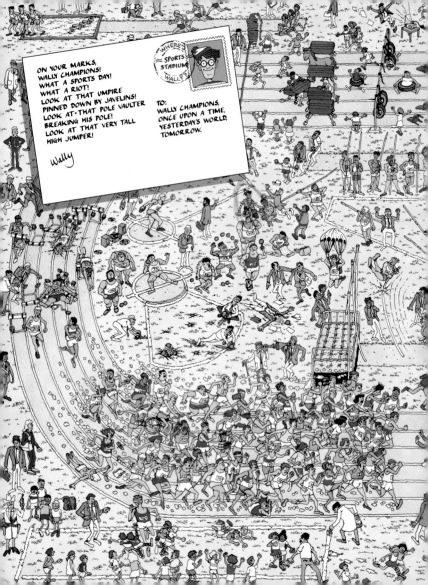

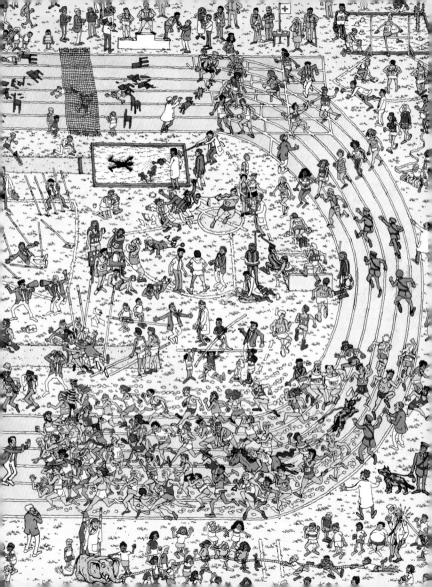

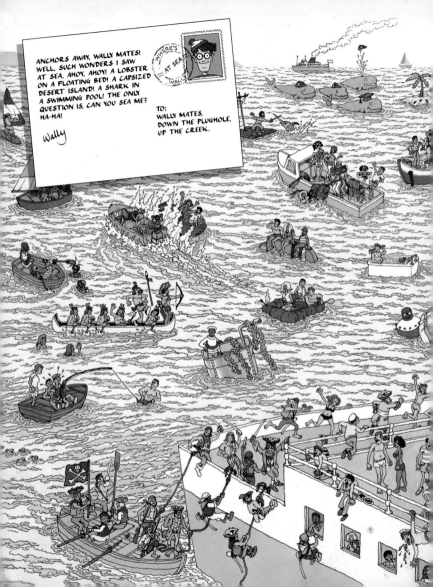

WATCH IT, WALLY HUNTERS!
I'M AN ANIMAL LOVER, THAT'S
FOR SURE. I LOVE THAT HIPPO
WITH ITS ALARM CLOCK; THAT
LION HAVING ITS MANE COMBED;
THE HAT-EATING GIRAFFE; THE
OWLS IN SPECTACLES. GREAT!

Wally

TO:
WALLY HUNTERS,
NICE PLACE,
THE JUNGLE,
OUTSIDE.

WHERE
SAFARI PARK
WALLY?

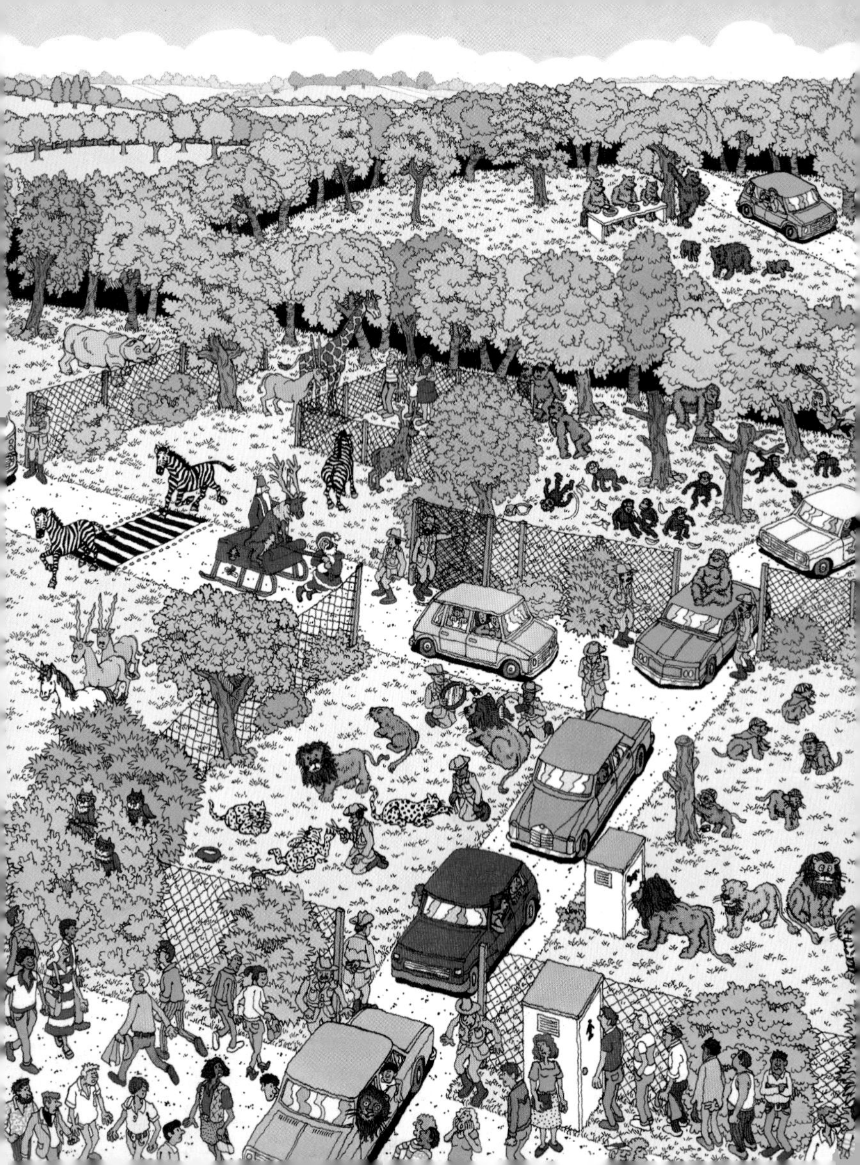

WOTCHA, WALLY-WATCHERS!
SAW SOME TRULY TERRIFIC
SIGHTS TODAY – SOMEONE
BURNING TROUSERS WITH
AN IRON; A LONG THIN MAN
WITH A LONG THIN TIE;
A GLOVE ATTACKING A MAN.
PHEW! INCREDIBLE!

Wally

TO:
WALLY-WATCHERS,
OVER THE MOON,
THE WILD WEST,
NOW.

WHERE
DEPARTMENT
STORE
WALLY?

THE GREAT WHERE'S WALLY? CHECKLIST
Hundreds more things for Wally-watchers to watch out for!

IN TOWN
- A dog on a roof
- A man on a fountain
- A man about to trip over a dog's lead
- A car crash
- A keen barber
- People in a street, watching TV
- A puncture caused by a Roman arrow
- A tearful tune
- A boy attacked by a plant
- A waiter who isn't concentrating
- A robber who's been clobbered
- A face on a wall
- A man coming out of a man-hole
- A man feeding pigeons
- A bicycle crash

SKI SLOPES
- A man reading on a roof
- A flying skier
- A runaway skier
- A backward skier
- A portrait in snow
- An illegal fisherman
- A snowball in the neck
- Two unconscious skiers
- Two skiers hitting trees
- An Alpine horn
- A snow skier
- A flag collector
- Two very scruffy skiers
- A skier up a tree
- A water skier on snow
- A Yeti
- A skiing reindeer
- A roof jumper
- A heap of skaters

THE RAILWAY STATION
- A boy falling from a train
- A break-down on tracks
- Naughty children on a train roof
- People being knocked over by a door
- A man about to step on a ball
- Three different times at the same time
- A wheelbarrow pram
- A face on a train
- Five people reading one newspaper
- A struggling bag carrier
- A show-off with suitcases
- A man losing everything from his cases
- A smoking train
- A squeeze on a bench
- Fare dodgers
- A dog tearing a man's trousers
- A hand caught between doors
- A cattle stampede
- A man breaking a weighing machine

ON THE BEACH
- A dog biting a boy's bottom
- A man who is overdressed
- A muscular medallion man
- A popular girl
- A water skier on water
- A stripy photo
- A punctured lilo
- A donkey who likes ice-cream
- A man being squashed
- A punctured beach ball
- A human pyramid
- A human stepping-stone
- Two odd friends
- A cowboy
- A human donkey
- Age and beauty
- A boy who follows in his father's footsteps
- Two men with vests, one without
- A boy being tortured by a spider
- A show-off with sandcastles
- A gang of hat robbers
- An Arab making pyramids
- Three protruding tongues
- Two oddly fitting hats
- An odd couple
- Five sprinters
- A towel with a hole in it
- A punctured hovercraft
- A boy who's not allowed any ice-cream

CAMP SITE
- A bull in a hedge
- Bull horns
- A shark in a canal
- A bull seeing red
- A careless kick
- Tea in a lap
- A low bridge
- People knocked over by a mallet
- A man surprised undressing
- A bicycle tyre about to be punctured
- Camper's camels
- A scarecrow that doesn't work
- A wigwam
- Large biceps
- A collapsed tent
- A smoking barbecue
- A fisherman catching old boots
- A winning penny-farthing
- Boy scouts making fire
- A roller hiker
- A man blowing up a boat
- A camper's butler
- Runners on the road
- A bull chasing children
- Scruffy campers
- Thirsty walkers

SPORTS STADIUM
- Three pairs of feet, sticking out of sand
- A cowboy starting races
- Hopeless hurdlers
- Ten children with fifteen legs
- A record thrower
- A shot-put juggler
- An ear trumpet
- A vaulting horse
- A runner with two wheels
- A parachuting vaulter
- A Scotsman with a caber
- An elephant pulling a rope
- People being knocked over by a hammer
- A gardener
- Three frogmen
- A runner without any shorts on
- A bed
- A bandaged boy
- A runner with four legs
- A sunken jumper
- A man with an odd pair of legs
- A man chasing a dog, chasing a cat
- A boy squirting water

MUSEUM

- A very big skeleton
- A clown squirting water
- A catapult firing a child
- A bird's nest in a woman's hair
- A highwayman
- A popping bicep
- An arrow in the neck
- A knight watching TV
- Picture robbers
- A smoking picture
- A leaking watercolour
- Fighting pictures
- A king and queen
- A fat picture and a thin one
- Three cave men
- A game of catch with a bomb
- Charioteers
- A collapsing pillar

SAFARI PARK

- Noah's Ark
- A message in a bottle
- A hippo having its teeth cleaned
- A bird's nest in an antler
- A hungry giraffe
- An ice-cream robber
- A zebra crossing
- Father Christmas
- Three owls
- A unicorn
- Caged people
- A lion driving a car
- Bears
- Tarzan
- Lion cubs
- An Indian tiger
- Two queues for the toilets
- Animals' beauty parlour
- An elephant squirting water

DEPARTMENT STORE

- An ironing demonstration
- A woman surprised undressing
- A man whose boots face the wrong way
- A man with heavy shopping
- A misbehaving vacuum cleaner
- Ties that match their wearers
- A man washing his clothes
- A man trying on a jacket that's too big
- A woman tripping over toys
- A boy pulling a girl's hair
- A boy riding in a shopping trolley
- A glove that's alive

AT SEA

- A windsurfer
- A boat punctured by an arrow
- A sword fight with a swordfish
- A school of whales
- Seasick sailors
- A leaking diver
- A boat crash
- A bathtub
- A seabed
- A game of noughts and crosses
- A lucky fisherman
- Three lumberjacks
- Unlucky fishermen
- Two water skiers in a tangle
- Fish robbers
- A sea cowboy
- A fishy photo
- A man being strangled by an octopus
- Stowaways
- A Chinese junk
- A wave at sea

FAIRGROUND

- A cannon at a rifle range
- A bumper car run wild
- A sword swallower
- A one-armed bandit
- A boy balloonist
- A runaway fairground rocket
- A runaway fairground horse
- A haunted house
- Seven lost children and a lost dog
- A tank crash
- A weightlifter dropping his weights
- Three clowns
- Three men dressed as bears

AIRPORT

- A flying saucer
- A boy who's been hiding in a suitcase
- A child firing a catapult
- A leaking fuel pipe
- Flight controllers playing badminton
- A rocket
- A turret
- Three watch smugglers
- Naughty children on a plane
- A forklift truck
- A wind-sock
- A chopper
- A plane that doesn't fly
- A flying Ace
- Dracula
- Five men blowing up a balloon
- Runners on a runway
- Four smoking people
- Four people falling from a plane
- A cargo of cattle
- A fire engine
- Three childish pilots
- An airship being punctured

WOW! WHAT A SEARCH!

Did you find Wally, all his friends, and all the things they lost? Did you find the one scene where Wally and Odlaw both lost their binoculars? Odlaw's binoculars are the ones nearest to him. Did you find the extra character who appears in every scene? If not, keep looking! Wow! Fantastic!

WHERE'S WALLY?

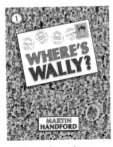

Down the road, over
the sea, around the globe…
Where's Wally? on his
worldwide adventures! Terrific!

Over thousands of years,
past thousands of people…
Where's Wally? *now*!
Amazing!

Once upon a mermaid,
once upon a dragon…
Where's Wally? in the
realms of fantasy! Magic!

Lights, camera, action…
Where's Wally? behind the
scenes! Cool!

Stepping off the pages, and
into life… Where's Wally?
in lands full of wonder! Wow!

Pick a sticker, spot the
difference, match the
silhouettes… Where's Wally?
at the gallery! Brilliant!

Have you found all six Wally books yet?